CRAFTY HALLOWEEN PUMPKINS

by CLARE BEATON

PUMPKIN CAKE

Dark ginger cake

A delicious cake which keeps well.

What you will need to make the cake:

★ 9 tablespoons treacle
★ 60 g demerara sugar
★ 135 g butter
★ 250 g plain flour
★ 3 level teaspoons ground ginger
★ 1 1/2 level teaspoons mixed spice
★ 3/4 level teaspoon bicarbonate of soda
★ 3 eggs, beaten
★ 6 tablespoons milk

Ask an adult to help melt the ingredients and put the tray in and out of the oven.

Before you start, put on an apron and wash your hands.

You will also need:

★ greaseproof paper
★ 25 cm round cake tin
★ small saucepan
★ wooden spoon
★ sieve
★ mixing bowl
★ cooling rack
★ knife for trimming cake

Lining the cake tin:
When you line the bottom of a cake tin, put the tin on the greaseproof paper and draw round it. Cut the paper just inside the line. Put the paper in the bottom of the tin.

Grease and line the bottom of the cake tin with greaseproof paper.

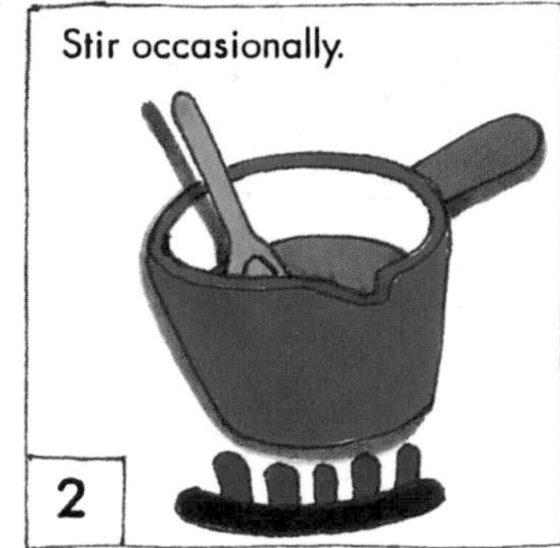

Gently heat the treacle, sugar and butter in the small pan until melted.

Sift the flour, spices and bicarbonate of soda into the mixing bowl.

Pour the melted mixture over the dry ingredients. Add the eggs and milk. Beat until smooth.

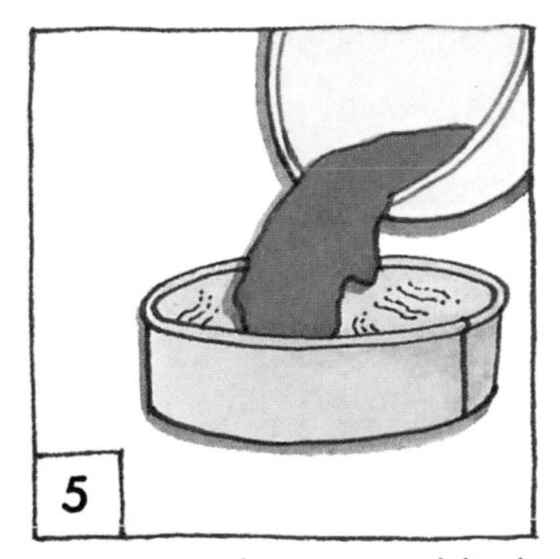

Pour into the tin and bake in the oven at 170°C/ 325°F or Gas 3 for about 1¼ hours.

When cool, trim the cake into a pumpkin shape. Turn to page 4 to decorate.

Butter icing

What you will need:

- ★ 100 g butter
- ★ 225 g icing sugar
- ★ 1-2 tablespoons milk
- ★ few drops of orange food colouring

You will also need:

- ★ mixing bowl
- ★ wooden spoon
- ★ sieve
- ★ knife

Put the butter in the mixing bowl and beat it until soft.

A little at a time, beat in sifted icing sugar, milk and colouring.

Sprinkle your work surface with a little icing sugar. Roll out the marzipan.

Cut three triangles for the eyes and nose. Cut a big mouth.

Pumpkin face

What you will need:

- ★ 1 tablespoon icing sugar
- ★ 85 g marzipan

You will also need:

- ★ rolling-pin
- ★ knife
- ★ tin foil
- ★ sticky tape
- ★ scissors

Cut a piece of tin foil 86 cm long, and fold into a 4.5 cm wide strip. Cut a fringe along one edge 1 cm deep. Wrap around cake folding fringe down. Tape end.

PUMPKIN CARDS

What you will need:

- ★ thick orange paper or thin card
- ★ pencil
- ★ scissors
- ★ black pen, crayon or paint
- ★ thin shiny gift ribbon
- ★ sticky tape

Party invitations

Make these pumpkin cards to invite your friends to a Halloween or any autumn party. Put them into an envelope and add a sticker or two.

Use gold, silver or any other coloured ribbon.

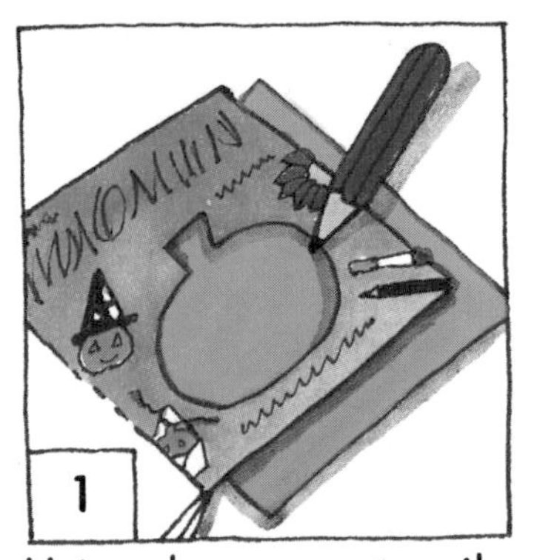

Using the cover stencil, draw pumpkins on the orange paper or card. Cut out.

Draw the face on one side in black pen, crayon or paint.

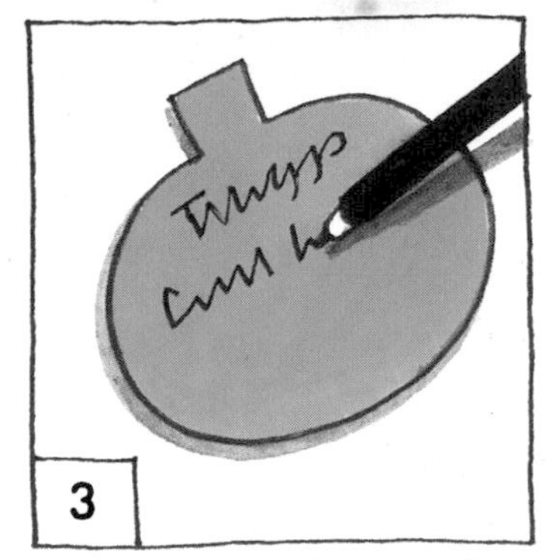

Turn over and write the details of the party (see below).

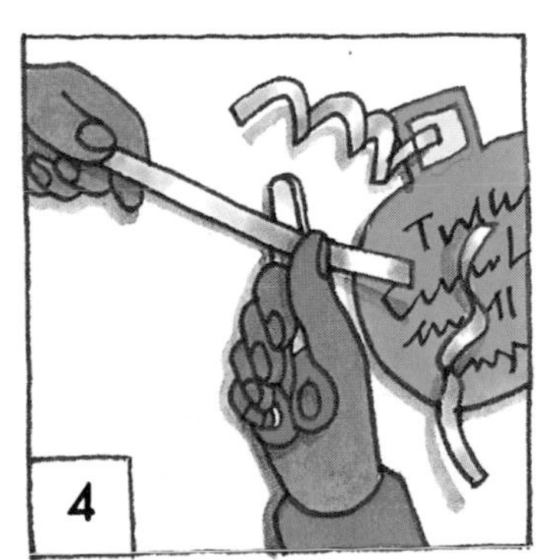

Curl the ribbon by pulling along closed scissors and tape on to the pumpkin stalk.

Pumpkin place cards

Make sure your party guests know their place! Fold the orange card or paper in half. Place the cover stencil so the top of the stalk is on the fold. Then follow steps 1 and 2 on page 7.

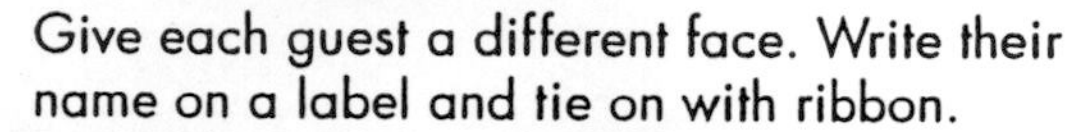

Give each guest a different face. Write their name on a label and tie on with ribbon.

DON'T BE SCARED
HAPPY HALLOWEEN
HAPPY HALLOWEEN
Whoooooooooo
COME TO MY PARTY

DON'T BE LATE!

BOO!

BEWARE!

PUMPKIN PIN CUSHION

This makes a lovely gift for anyone who enjoys sewing. Choose the pumpkin fabric carefully. It can be orange or yellow. Stripes look great but must run from top to bottom.

What you will need:

★ strip of fabric 28 cm x 12 cm
★ small piece of green felt
★ pins and needle
★ coloured threads
★ scissors
★ toy stuffing
★ tracing paper
★ pencil

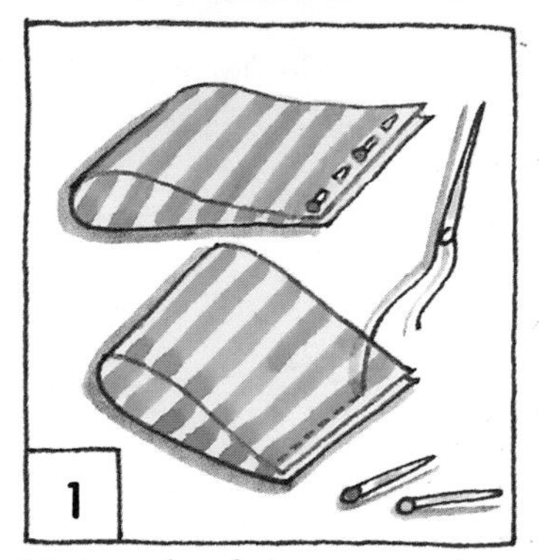

Using the fabric inside out, pin and sew the short sides together 1 cm from the edge.

Sew along one long side 1 cm from the edge. Then pull the stitching until it is tight.

Turn the fabric right side out. Stuff it until it is nice and fat.

Stitch along the top edge, 1 cm from the edge. Pull tight and fasten with a knot.

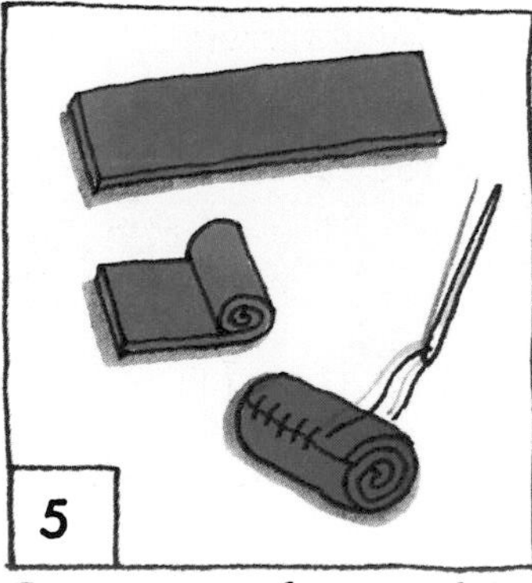

Cut a strip of green felt 10 cm x 2 cm for the stalk. Roll up tightly and sew together.

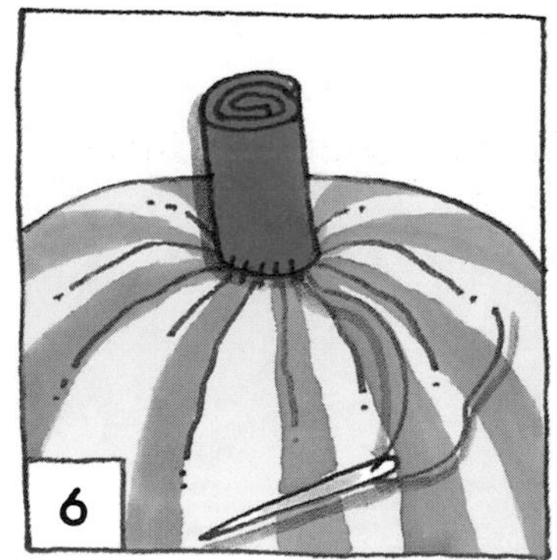

Place on top of the pumpkin on the gathered end. Sew it on.

Now make the leaf. Use tracing paper and trace the template below. Pin on to green felt.

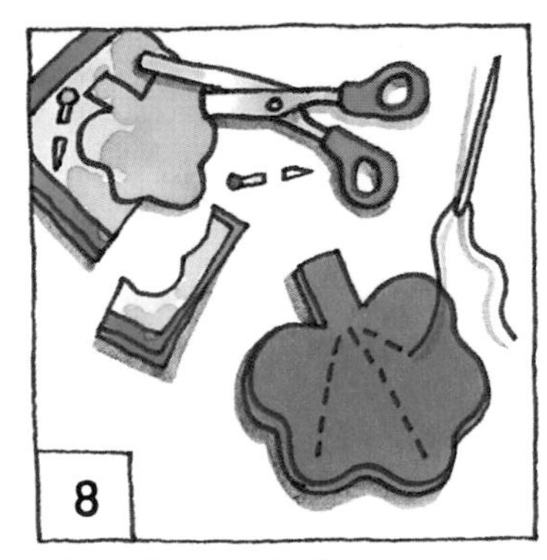

Cut through the paper and felt. Remove the paper. Sew veins on the leaf in green stitching.

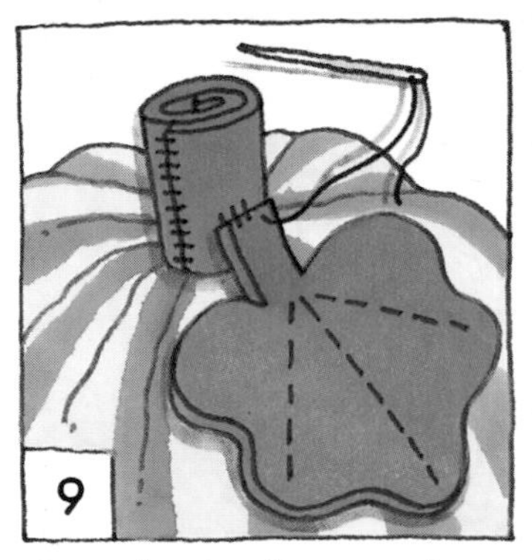

Sew the leaf on to the bottom of the stalk.

Leaf template

Dotted lines show where to stitch veins.

Try different colour fabrics.

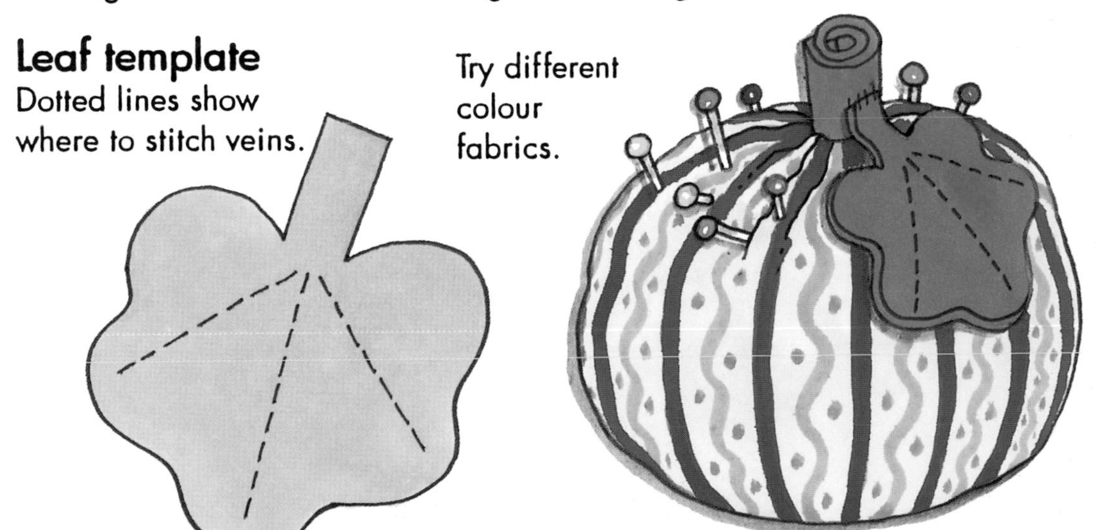

PUMPKIN FACES

Decorate your home with these jolly pumpkin faces.

Table decoration

Draw faces on satsumas or oranges with black felt-tip pens. Pile up on a plate.

Window decoration

Using the cover stencil draw pumpkins on to orange paper. Cut out and draw faces in black felt-tip pen.

Sticky tape the pumpkins on to lengths of black wool, string or strong thread. Hang up in windows.

PUMPKIN CLOAK

Wear this at a Halloween party or whilst trick or treating.

What you will need:

★ black plastic bin bag
★ orange paper
★ pencil and scissors
★ black felt-tip pen
★ glue

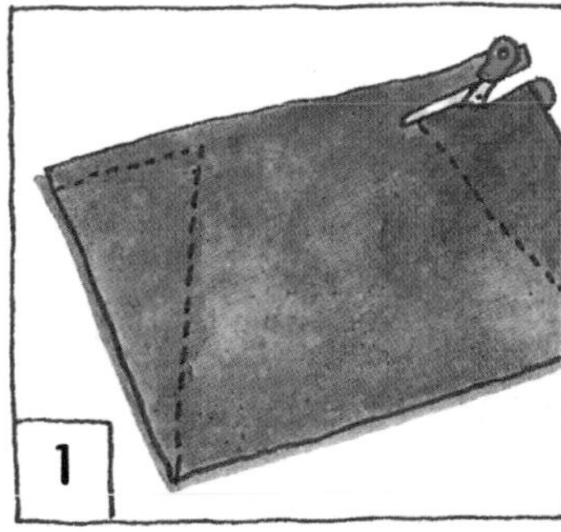

1

Cut bin liner along two sides. Open out and cut into cloak shape with neck tie.

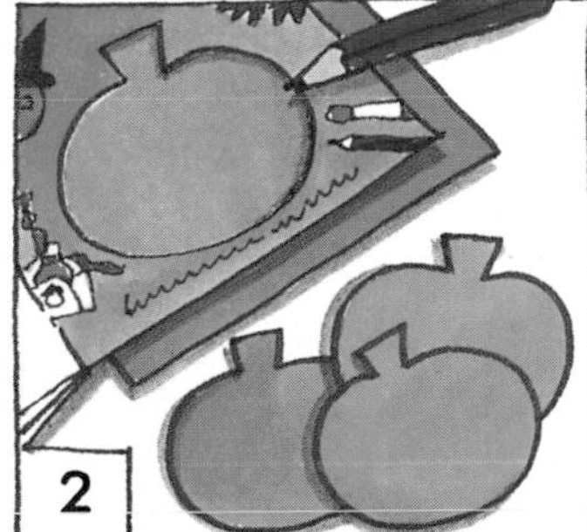

2

Place cover stencil on orange paper. Draw round shape with pencil and cut out several.

3

Draw faces on to paper pumpkins with black pen. Glue all over one side of plastic cloak.

PARTY PUMPKINS

Orange pumpkins look terrific on a black background.

Using the cover stencil cut out lots of orange paper pumpkins. Draw faces on them in black felt-tip pen. Stick and tie them all over yourself!

Headband

Tape on to wool and tie around your head.

Necklace and bracelet

Tape on to black wool.

Pumpkin torch

Cut face out and tape on to the end of a torch.

Face paint

Draw eyes, nose and mouth in black.

PUMPKIN SEED NECKLACE

Make these colourful necklaces with pumpkin seeds and nail varnish. Remove the seeds from a pumpkin and wash thoroughly under the cold tap. Leave to dry spread out on a tray or in a warm place.

What you will need:

★ clean, dry pumpkin seeds
★ plasticine
★ different coloured nail varnish
★ darning needle
★ thread

WARNING
Always check with a grown-up before using nail varnish. It has a strong smell so use in a well-ventilated room.

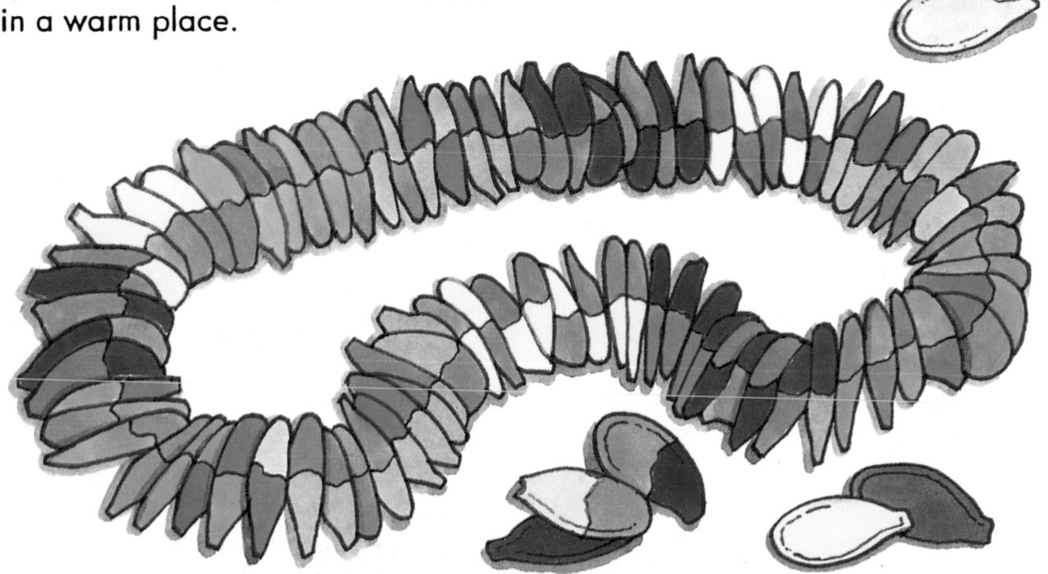

1

Stick the seeds into plasticine to hold them steady. Colour the top half of the seed with nail varnish.

2

When dry, turn the seeds over and paint the other half in the same or a contrasting colour.

Knot the ends of the thread.
3

Use a needle with double thread knotted at the end. Push through the centre of the seeds. Carry on threading until the necklace is long enough.

Shake the bottles before using.

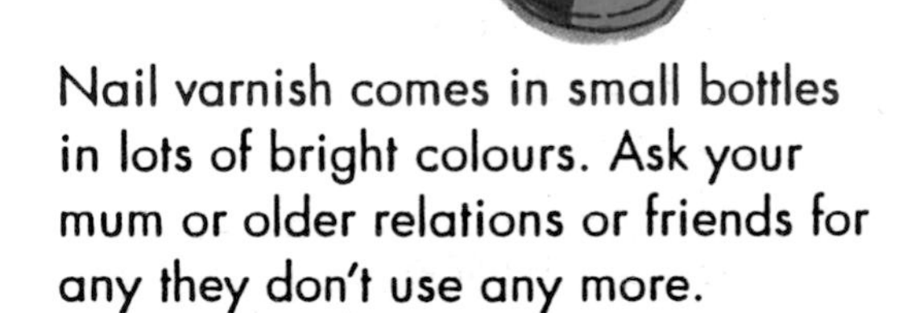

Nail varnish comes in small bottles in lots of bright colours. Ask your mum or older relations or friends for any they don't use any more.